Hugging the Rock

Hugging the Rock

Susan Taylor Brown

Tricycle Press
Berkeley | Toronto

Tricycle Press
an imprint of Ten Speed Press
PO Box 7123
Berkeley, California 94707
www.tricyclepress.com

Book design by Chloe Rawlins
Cover illustration by Michael Morgenstern
Typeset in Adobe Garamond and Laricio

Library of Congress Cataloging-in-Publication Data
Brown, Susan Taylor, 1958-
   Hugging the rock / Susan Taylor Brown ; [cover illustration by
Michael Morgenstern].
      p. cm.
   Summary: Through a series of poems, Rachel expresses her
feelings about her parents' divorce, living without her mother, and
her changing attitude towards her father.
   ISBN 13: 978-1-58246-180-9 hc/ ISBN 13: 978-1-58246-236-3 pbk
   ISBN 10: 1-58246-180-5 hc/ ISBN 10: 1-58246-236-4 pbk
   [1. Mothers and daughters--Fiction. 2. Divorce--Fiction.
3. Fathers and daughters--Fiction. 4. Novels in verse.]   I. Title.
PZ7.B8179Hu 2006
   [Fic]--dc22

2006005738

First Tricycle Press printing, 2006
First paperback printing, 2008
Printed in USA
1 2 3 4 5 6 — 12 11 10 09 08

For my children, Ryan and Jennifer Olson,
who struggled with their own rocky stories.

And for my husband, Erik Giberson,
who helped me find myself when I was lost
and is a rock
the good kind
that I can always count on.

The First Day

No Room

When my mom decides to run away from home
she packs up her car
with all the things that matter most
to her.

Her guitar
and some books
all her CDs
her clothes
her shoes
Grandma's music box from the fireplace mantle
and the quilt from the bed she shares with Dad.

She jams plastic grocery bags
filled with soap and shampoo
into the small spaces
left in between things
and ties a couple of suitcases to the roof.
At the last minute she
throws in a few dishes
some towels

and a potted red geranium
that guards the front porch.

Dad tells her not to pack stuff too high
so she can still see out the back window
but she ignores him
and shoves her pillow
between her guitar case and the portable TV.

By the time she's done
there's no room left for anything else.
No room left for Dad.

And no room left for me.

The Wrong Answers

When I ask her why she's leaving
she finds lots of ways
to not answer me.

She yanks photos from the albums
and dumps out her purse on the kitchen table
then puts everything back in it again.
She unloads the dishwasher
just like any other day.

"Why do you have to go?"

Because I can't stay.

"Why?"

She paces
arms swinging wildly
trapped
like a bee in a jar.

I don't belong here anymore.

"If you're not supposed to be here
where are you supposed to be?"

I don't know, Rachel.
I just don't know.

"Why can't I go with you?"

You just can't.
Later
yes later
maybe after I get settled
but now
now you need to stay here
you have to stay with your dad
it will all be fine
even better than fine, I bet.

I don't mean to,
but I snort
and she slams her hand down
on the kitchen table.

I jump.

I can't do this anymore, Rachel!

I wonder
if she took her pills this morning
then I glance at the bottle
near the coffee pot
and she catches me looking.

Yes, she says.
But sometimes they don't work.

And then she starts to cry.

The Garage

I sit on a milk crate
and watch Dad
make sure Mom's car
is safe to drive.
First he adds some air to the front tires.
Then he pulls out the dipstick
wipes it clean with a rag
and shoves it back in again to check the oil.
He scrapes crud off the battery
then closes the hood.

I still can't believe this is really happening.

I peek in the windows of the car
too close
and leave an imprint of my face on the glass.

Stop that, hollers Dad.
Look at the mess you've made.

My faceprint
is stuck to the glass.

I should do it to every window
so she'll see me
following her even when she's gone.

Get some paper towels.

I squirt the cleaner and wipe it off
but I must not be fast enough
or good enough
because he takes the paper towel from my hand.

Never mind, he says. *I'll do it myself.*

Mom comes out
drops empty boxes on the floor
and glares at Dad.

I washed the car yesterday, she says.
Windows too.
Not clean enough for you?

She wants to fight;
I can tell.
Dad won't answer her

won't even look at her.
He just scrubs the window
harder and harder
until Mom gives up
and goes back in the house.

Run Away

I run away
fast.

Away
from Dad
hiding in his garage.

Away
from Mom
and her packed car.

Faster.

Past the mailbox.

Faster.

To the corner and back
again
again
again
like a relay race at school.

Mom's dog, Madison,
barks
and chases me
like it's a game
but it's not.

I run as fast as I can
but I can't run fast enough
to run away
from the idea of her leaving.

I collapse on the grass.
Madison sits down next to me
panting
and big drops of saliva hit my arm.
I let the drool slide down my elbow
before I wipe it off with the edge of my shirt
wishing I could wipe off today
as easy as that.

The Bargain

It's not fair
that a mom can just decide to leave
and a kid can't decide
to not let her go.

I'm sorry, Mom. I'm sorry.
Please don't go.
Please. I love you. Dad loves you.
Doesn't that count?
Whatever I did wrong, I'm sorry.
I won't do it anymore.

You said I could pierce my ears
and get a raise in my allowance.
You promised
I could finally have a kitten
of my very own
to sleep in my room.
Did you tell Dad about that?
I haven't started to shave my legs yet
and what if I get my period?
And does Dad even know where

to find the hot-water bottle
when I get sick?

I don't know how to talk to Dad.
He's too quiet
and I never know what he's thinking
and he's always gone at work.

What if he gets mad and leaves me too?

We can get you help.
More help. More something.
I know a girl whose mom felt bad all the time
and the mom went away to this hospital
for a while
and when she came home
she was better, mostly.

You could go there.

I thought you loved us. Loved me.
I'll be good. I promise.
Clean my room without being told
do all my homework

leave you alone
whenever you want quiet time.

Just please
please

don't go.

Questions

When I come home
Mom is upstairs
and Dad darts around the kitchen
with an orange sponge in his hand.
He scrubs the sink
wipes down the chrome faucet
then pushes all the chairs up to the table.

I want to ask him things
like
does he feel the same way I do right now
all mixed-up
and hurting
and mad
at the same time?
And does he have any idea
where she'll go
when we'll see her again
and what my life will be like
after she's gone?

He clutches the broom
sweeping long half-circles
that slowly bring him closer to me.

"Dad?"

He stops
looks up
but I don't think he really sees me
standing right in front of him.

We'll be okay, Rachel.
Everything will be okay.

He's wrong.
I know he's wrong.
Nothing will ever be okay again.

My Crowning Glory

I've always had long hair
just like my mom.

She calls it my crowning glory.

I braid it every night
or it's a mess of knots in the morning.

When I was little
I used to lie down on the kitchen counter
so she could wash my hair in the sink.
She'd roll up a towel for under my neck
make lots of suds
then rinse it again and again
with vinegar
until it was squeaky clean.

The entire time
she sang me bits of songs she wrote
about falling in love
taking chances
and getting your heart broken.

I'd sit on a stool in front of her
while she combed out the tangles
and told me my hair shimmered
like black pearls in the sun
and to never cut it
because it made me look just like a princess.

I'd tell her I wanted to live in a castle
with a moat
and a dungeon
and marry a prince
with a white horse
just like in the fairy tales.

Sometimes she'd play along
and pretend to be a queen
with a very tall crown
and sometimes
she'd tell me that
not every princess
needs a prince
and that life in a castle
didn't sound like much fun to her.

Final Instructions

Mind your father, she says.
Take care of Madison for me.
Eat your vegetables.

"I can do the first two," I say.
"I'm not so sure about the last one."

I have instructions of my own
but I don't say them out loud.

Take your pills every day.
Do whatever you need to do
and then come home soon.

Don't forget about me.

For Real

Dad and I follow her outside
to say good-bye.

A sour taste hits my mouth
and I want to puke
right there in the middle of our driveway.

She hugs Dad quick;
then, before I'm ready,
she stands in front of me.

Inside
I feel myself break
into a million pieces.

"Mom!" I cry
and rush into her arms.

She holds me,
but she holds me different
and now I know
that this is for real.

The Rock

Madison waits for an invitation
to jump into her usual spot
on the front seat of Mom's car.
Mom pushes her away
but Madison doesn't understand
and starts to bark.

Mom tells me again
my place is with Dad.
She tells me
someday I'll understand.

I look at Dad
who is trying hard not to look at Mom
as she gets ready to drive away.
He hugs his arms close to his chest
and sucks his bottom lip in over his teeth.
He wears what Mom calls his disappearing face
because when he wears it
all his feelings just disappear
and no one can tell what he's thinking.

I go stand next to him.
I want to hold his hand and have him hold mine
but that's not the way things work
with me and Dad.

I lean on him just a little
too much
and he steps away.
I wobble
back and forth
before I catch my balance.

Mom says he's a rock
the good kind you can always count on
to do the right thing.

It's hard for me to think of a rock
as something good.
Some rocks are heavy
and make you sink.
Some rocks are too big to move.
And some rocks are sharp
and cut you
if you try to hold them in your hand.

Good-bye

When she finally drives away
I realize that Mom is a rock too,
the kind that crumbles
if you hold on too tight.

Blame

I didn't think she'd really go
but she did
and I clench my fists
until my nails dig into my skin
and the mad I've been holding back
breaks free.

I turn on Dad.

"It's your fault.
I know it is. It's all your fault."

It's no one's fault.
I'm sorry, Rachel. Things happen.
Even when we don't want them to.

It has to be his fault.
It has to.

My face feels hot
and red
and I know I'm going to cry again

even though I shouldn't
have any tears left
in me at all.
I can't stop shouting at him.

"You did something to make her leave.
I know you did!"

He doesn't say anything else.
He just waits,
wearing his disappearing face
while Mom disappears down the road.

Why didn't he try to make her stay?
Why didn't he do something?

Maybe he wanted her to go.
Maybe he made her go.

I push the thought down as soon as it comes
but the doubt is there
and that makes me even madder.

"I hate you! I hate you! I hate you!"

He just stands there
with his hands jammed in his pockets
and lets me yell at him
until I'm all yelled out.

No No No

He sits on the couch
staring at me
sitting on the floor
staring anywhere but
back at him.

Homework?

"No."

Hungry?

"No."

Do you want to watch TV?

"No!"

I stand up
to escape to my room.
He catches my hand
as I rush by.

Don't be mad at your mother, Rachel.

I pull my hand away from his,
fast.

"I'm not," I say.
"I'm mad at you."

I Don't Remember

I don't remember much
from when I was really little
but I'm pretty sure
I was happy.

Me.
Mom.
Dad.
My family.

I don't remember
the first time
Mom stayed up all night
or the first time
she shopped so much
for things we didn't need
that Dad took away her credit cards.

I don't remember
when making sure Mom took her pills
became the first thing I did
every morning

or when Dad decided to work late
every night
or when I began spending
more time
at Sara's house
than I did at home.

I don't remember when I figured out
it was easier to keep my thoughts on the
inside
instead of sharing them.
Easier to want
whatever Mom wanted.
Easier to pretend
like Dad
that everything was all right
instead of talking
about everything that was all wrong.

I don't remember when
our family started to
fall apart.

The First Week

Grandma to the Rescue

When I get home from school
Grandma stands at the sink
peeling potatoes for dinner.

She gives me a hug hello.

There's clean laundry to fold, she says.
But do your homework first.

She takes Mom's notes
off the refrigerator door
and throws them in the garbage.

I pull them out
and put them back where they belong.

That dog should be in the yard, she says.
There's dog hair everywhere.

She opens the back door,
waving Madison outside.

I let Madison back in
dig a doggie treat out of the box
and give it to her
without making her do a single trick.

This house is a shambles, she says.
Time for a good cleaning.

The smell of lemon
fills the house
then Grandma
rearranges the furniture in the living room
and puts Dad's favorite chair
too far away to see the TV.

"Why is she doing this?" I ask him
as soon as he comes home.

She wants to help, says Dad.

At dinner
Grandma tries to make me eat
the mountain of peas
she piles on my plate

but I say I'm not hungry
and ask to go to my room.

Instead
I hide in the hall
and listen.

I told you not to marry her, says Grandma.
I knew she had problems.
Big problems.

Shush, says Dad.

Too late.
I already heard.

In the morning
the living room is back to normal
and Grandma's suitcase
waits by the front door.

Sara

I met Sara in the first grade
when a big second-grader took my lunch
and she made him give it back.

In third grade
I had the chicken pox.
No field trip to the zoo
for me.
Sara said she felt sick too
then convinced her mom
to take us to see the lions and tigers
by ourselves.

Sara gets in trouble
for making jokes in class
or imitating our teacher's voice
when she takes roll.

I don't like when people stare at me
point
or call out my name
so everyone will look.

Sara always dreams up
crazy things for us to do.

Once we swapped moms
without telling them.

I spent the day at Sara's house
pretending Sara's mom was my mom.
We made birdhouses for the garden
and when I slipped up
and called her "Mom" out loud
she smiled.

Sara went to my house
ready to play make-believe
but my mom had stopped taking her pills.

She was making cookies
and Sara helped
until there were dozens and dozens
all over the kitchen table
and the counter
and on top of the TV in the living room

and even in the laundry room
on the washer and dryer.

When Sara asked
why she needed so many cookies
my mom burst into tears
and dumped them all in the garbage.
Then she locked Sara out of the house.

I can't trade moms with Sara anymore
but I can show up at her house
and tell her I've been locked out
and she understands.

The Ring

I have a nightmare
that Dad runs away next
and leaves me and Madison
alone
to take care of each other.

I go downstairs for hot chocolate
the kind you make with hot water.
Madison follows me.

I stop when I see
the light on in the kitchen
hold Madison by the collar
and wait.

Dad sits at the table
and slides his wedding ring
up and down his finger.
He pulls it off
and clenches it in his fist.

Madison bumps me
and I realize I'm holding her too tight.
I let go just as he drops the ring.
It falls
spins in a circle
then comes to rest in front of him.
He makes a sound, almost a cry,
then slaps the ring with his hand
sending it flying off the table
onto the floor
and it rolls
under the stove.

I tug at Madison
until she follows me
back to my room
and curls up next to me
on my bed.

In the morning
I use a wooden spoon
to slide the ring out from under the stove.

I hide it in a sock
and tuck it under my mattress.
I know it's my imagination
but I think I feel it
poke me
every time I roll over in bed.

Dad Goes Grocery Shopping

Dad goes grocery shopping
on his way home from work
and fills the cupboards
with cans of spaghetti and chili
and the freezer
with frozen chicken dinners
that neither of us wants to eat.

He buys the wrong kind of dog food
forgets the toilet paper
and the milk
and has to go back to the store.

When he gets home
he sees Mom's grocery list
(in alphabetical order)
hidden behind the coupons
(ripped from the newspaper)
stuck to the refrigerator
and he kicks the toilet paper
across the room.

My New Life

The first week
I don't tell Sara
that Mom left us.
I don't lie
not really.
When she wants to come over
I say no
because no one's home.
When she asks about my mom
I shrug my shoulders
and ask about our homework.

The first week
Dad tries to do the laundry.
He puts my red shirt
in with the white towels
and everything turns pink.
He calls Grandma
and she tells him
not to mix colors with whites.

I could have told him that.

The first week
he tells me he'll leave a note
with a list of chores
he expects me to do
every day
before he gets home from work.

The first week
I spend most of the time
I'm supposed to be doing chores
in my room with Madison
wondering what I did
so wrong
that my mom had to run away.

Madison

Madison won't eat.

Dad buys canned dog food
with juicy gravy
and bits of turkey
but she just lies on the floor near her bowl
and starves herself.

I remember when Mom brought Madison home
from the pet store
that kept her in a cage
with too many other dogs.

Mom didn't want Madison to bite me
so she filled Madison's bowl with food
then we sat on the floor next to her.
While she ate
Mom stuck her hand in the bowl
took dog food out
then put it back again
to show Madison it was okay.

Madison was just a puppy
and thought it was a game
licking the food
from our fingers
like she was eating an ice-cream cone.

I stretch out on the floor
next to Madison.
Her stomach growls
and I know it's empty.
I can't remember when she last ate.

I squish my fingers in the wet dog food
and hold my hand under her nose.

"You have to eat," I say.

I wait.

The dog food stinks and
some of it slides down my hand
and plops on the floor.

I keep waiting.

Her whiskers move.
Her nose twitches.

I wait a long time before her tongue
finally touches my finger.
For over an hour
I dip my fingers in the sticky food
feeding it to Madison
until her bowl is empty.

Outside In

It's only been a week
but it seems like much longer.

On the outside
I look the same.
I eat breakfast
feed Madison
go to school.
I tell Sara I can't hang out with her
but I still don't tell her why.

On the inside
things are different.
I have a stomachache that never goes away
bad dreams wake me in the night
and I want to scream about everything.

But I don't cry.

Mom used to cry
then Mom fell apart
and now she's gone.

If I cry
everyone will know how I feel.

Then what?

The Stranger

He tries to help
by making my lunch,
sandwiches with not enough jelly
apples that I never eat.
(Shouldn't he know I like bananas best?)
He doesn't write my name on the bag
like Mom used to do
even though I was way too old for it.

After school
flowers plucked from the yard
wait for him to say how nice they look
in their vase.
He just heats up a can of chili for dinner
and hands me a bowl.

I do my homework.
He pays the bills.
I don't ask him to quiz me on my spelling words.
He doesn't ask to check my math.

He calls good night
when I walk down the hall to bed.

I don't answer.

Later, when I'm supposed to be asleep,
I hear his footsteps.
I close my eyes and
pretend to snore.
The steps stop beside my bed
his fingers brush my face
I hold my breath.

I almost want to open my eyes
and ask for a hug
but hugging is still hard for both of us.

I wait
and try to be a rock.

He tugs the covers up snug,
like I was a little kid,
touches my face once more
then walks away.

I let myself sink into dreams
where mothers
and fathers
and daughters
all live happily ever after.

The First Month

Hunger

Most of the time we eat out
in restaurants where they actually
show you to your table
take your order
and keep your water glass full.

I always order for myself
whatever I want.
Once I ordered two hot-fudge sundaes
but no dinner
just to see what would happen.
The waiter brought me an ice cream feast
with hot fudge
whipped cream
and colored sprinkles on top.
I dipped a spoon in each one
and shoved them both in my mouth at once.

He didn't even notice.

Tonight we go to a new Chinese restaurant
instead of our regular one downtown.

He lets me pick out just the meat
and leave the vegetables behind.
He even gives me both fortune cookies.
I stick one in my pocket
to share with Madison.

On the way home
I throw up in the car.

I think he's mad
because he drives home so fast
but then he helps me inside
and makes a bed for me on the couch.
He brings the pink bucket
Mom always gave me when I was sick
and tells Madison
she can sit on the couch with me
just this once.
He even finds the heating pad.

Later I hear him on the phone to Grandma.

Rachel's sick. I don't know what to do.
Should I take her to the hospital?

I could get up and tell him I'm okay
I just ate too much too fast and
I feel better already.
But I like the idea of him worrying about me.
And I like the way he still needs his mom.

So I just cuddle up closer
to Madison
and don't say a word.

School

Every morning
Sara meets me at the corner
so we can walk to school together.
We've been best friends
forever
and I've never kept a secret from her
until now.
I want to tell her
except telling her
will make it more real.

Instead I tell her my mom is sick
and when she doesn't ask any more questions
I figure I still didn't lie to her.
Not really.

The teacher puts the homework on the board.
I don't write it down.
When she gives a surprise quiz on our spelling words
I leave most of the lines blank.
In P.E. I tell the teacher I twisted my ankle
so I sit on the bench

and watch everyone else run relays
which used to be my favorite thing to do.

After school
I hang out in the cafeteria
watching Sara rehearse for the play.
She plays the lead,
of course.

Instead of writing my book report
I make a list of all the reasons
I think my mom might have left.

Sara wants to read it
and tries to snatch my notebook.
I rip out the page
and shove it in my back pocket.

This time I do lie to her
and say it was just a note to a boy.

The Crush

Just tell me, says Sara.
I can help. You know I can.
It's Nathan, isn't it?

I shake my head.

Todd? I bet it's Todd.
He always picks you first for relays.

"He picks me first because I run fast."

Then who? I'm your best friend.
I should know everything about you.

I gulp hard and try not to think about
all the things
that Sara doesn't know about me
now.

She waits
with her stubborn face

that tells me she won't go anywhere
until I tell her what she wants.

"Sammy," I say.
His name slips out before I can stop it.

At first she doesn't say anything
and I think she'll drop it
but she doesn't.

Sammy? My brother Sammy?

She laughs
only it's not the kind of laugh you make
when you're happy.

*Fine. If you don't want to tell me
just say so.*

Reasons Mom Left

1. ~~Dad yelled at her.~~
2. ~~I got a bad grade in math.~~
3. ~~Dad didn't make enough money.~~
4. ~~I didn't keep my room clean.~~
5. ~~Dad made jokes about her cooking.~~
6. ~~I wouldn't eat my vegetables.~~
7. ~~Madison barked too much.~~
8. ~~Dad wasn't a good husband.~~
9. ~~I wasn't a good daughter.~~
10. I don't know.

Ghosts

Most mornings
he's gone before I get up.
He calls out to make sure I'm awake
then disappears before I'm dressed.

Most mornings
I eat cold cereal
and dig clean underwear out of the laundry basket.

Most nights
he turns on the TV
and flips channels every few minutes.

Most nights
I go to my room
and pretend to do my homework
or lay on my bed with Madison
and try not to think of anything at all.

Just Because

My teacher makes me stay in at recess

just because
I didn't do a book report

just because
I didn't finish my math

just because
I didn't even try to run when we played dodge ball.

I do word problems at my desk
after everyone else leaves
and promise to write the book report this weekend
even though I haven't read the book yet.

She asks me,
Is everything okay at home?

But I can't tell her anything about that.

Just because.

The Fight

Tonight when he comes home
Madison runs to meet him
and knocks over the kitchen garbage
where I left it
by the back door.

Coffee grinds
eggshells
wet newspaper
spill out on the floor
just as he walks in.

He yells.
Loud.

Rachel! Why didn't you take out the garbage?

"I forgot."

Didn't you read the list?

I did
but I don't tell him that.

"I just forgot."

Rachel, you HAVE to help me!
I can't do this alone.
I need you.

I don't believe
the rock needs anyone
but when I look at him
I don't see a rock
and for some reason
that makes me even madder
so I yell back at him.

"What about what I need?"

Mom's leaving is
right there in the kitchen
between us
like a pile of stinking garbage
and we yell back and forth

about everything
but Mom
until he says he's sorry.

I think he's sorry for Mom's leaving.
Instead he says he's sorry
he's not a very good father
and that he let Mom
keep him from getting close to me.

I want to know more
about how Mom kept him from me
but he says later.

After I pick up the garbage
I call Sara
and tell her that Mom left us.
She asks me
if I want her to ask her mom
if I can move in with them.
At first I say no
then maybe
then I tell her to ask me again in a few weeks.

What I Need

Grandma calls every day
to check up on me
then she talks to Dad
about all the things she thinks he's doing wrong.

Grandma tells him
I need to go to bed early.

Dad says
I need more time to adjust.

Grandma tells him
I need to quit biting my nails.

Dad says
I need to work things out my own way.

Grandma tells him
I need to go outside for some fresh air.

Dad says
I need time to relax.

Maybe I need those things
but I think I need something else
more.

Contact

I wait
and wait
and wait
for her first phone call
and when it finally comes
I can't think of anything to say.

Rachel? Rachel, are you there?

I nod several times
before I remember to say yes out loud.

"Where are you?" I ask.

It doesn't matter.

It does to me, but I don't want to fight.

I wait some more
until I get brave enough to ask
what I'm most afraid to ask.

"When can I come see you?"

Not yet, she says.

And then she hangs up
before I can ask her anything else.

Starring Rachel

Sara likes to talk about Mom's leaving
like it's a movie on TV
and I'm the star
and she's the star's best friend.

Scene one:
Picture a normal family.

Scene two:
Follow the girl
as she pretends everything's fine
even though it's not.

Scene three:
Move in for a close-up
of the girl,
tragic and lost.

No matter how many retakes we do
it always ends the same way.

If this were a movie
we'd have a script telling us what to say
and at the end
the mother would realize her mistake
and come running back home
just before the director says
cut.

Noises

Mom made
most of the noises
in our house,
the good ones and the bad ones.

For days she whistled when she cooked
sang when she did laundry
or hummed
when she looked over my shoulder
to check my homework.
Sometimes she laughed
and the sound felt so warm
as if the house had no roof
and the sunshine could just pour inside.

Then without warning
she'd spend all her time
up in their bedroom
alone
but she'd say nothing was wrong.

Other days
she cried and cried about things
she said we wouldn't understand.
Even with my door shut tight
and my pillow over my head
I could hear her.

If she couldn't sleep
she'd come to my room
bouncing on the edge of my bed
to wake me.

Fun
at first
drinking hot chocolate together
while Dad snored down the hall
but after three nights in a row
I was too tired for school.

When I told her I wanted to sleep,
she swept her arm across my dresser
and sent everything crashing to the floor.

She started driving
in the middle of the night instead.

Even now
I wake up
waiting
to hear her climb back up the stairs.

Searching

Madison wanders the house
sniffing the path that Mom used to walk
from the bedroom
down the hall
to the kitchen
and back to the bedroom once more.

Her nails tap the hardwood floor
and remind me of Mom
picking the strings on her guitar
on nights when she sat outside
to sing to the stars.

I look in the closet
and come across a pair of Mom's high heels
lost behind a box of my old baby clothes.
I slip them on and click my heels
like Dorothy's red shoes
and wait for the magic to bring her home.

Madison rubs her nose along the edge of the bed
searching for the leftover smell of her best friend.

She whimpers
then looks at me as though it's my fault
Mom's gone.

I feel so awful
I dig through the closet
for a shirt Mom left behind
and try to give it to Madison.
She sniffs it once then turns away
and I know just how she feels.

I kick off the shoes
and watch them fly across the room.
There is no magic
and I don't think she's ever coming back.

We Go Grocery Shopping Together

"Madison needs dog food," I say.

"The freezer's empty.
I need lunch for school.
There's no toilet paper
and you're all out of coffee."

The coffee got his attention.

At the store he grabs a carry basket
the kind you use for 10 items or less.
I grab the other basket
the kind you push.
We stand side by side like we're waiting
for the gun to fire
and the race to begin.
I hurry down the aisle.
There's a special on cans of spaghetti
and I dump a dozen in the cart.
I'm sick of canned spaghetti but I add more anyway.

I run to catch up with him
as he heads toward the meat.

He picks up a package of hamburger
thinks about it
then puts it back.

"I think I could make Mom's meat loaf.
Just some of that meat
and some bread
and some eggs."
I wait to see if I said the right thing.
"Or real spaghetti with big meatballs."

He takes a can from the cart
and makes a face
when he reads the ingredients.

We can do better than this, he says.

I nod and he tosses packages of meat into my cart
faster than I can take out the spaghetti.
It's like someone popped new batteries in him
and he's off
rushing toward the fruits and vegetables.

When he reaches for a bag of apples
and looks at me
I slowly shake my head.
He points to the oranges.
I shake my head again
and glance at the heap of bananas.

His eyes light up
and he charges around the aisle
pointing to grapes and pineapples and plums
until I'm shaking my head so fast
I see stars.

He smiles then
just a quick smile,
like it's something he's not used to doing,
then he puts a giant bunch of bananas in the cart.

As we head for the checkout stand
he reaches for my hand.
His fingers tuck between mine
like they know just where to go.
I'm surprised they're soft and warm
and not hard like a rock at all.

Kitchen Experiments

Dad buys a cookbook
and starts coming home early from work
so we can make dinner together.

The first night
after our baked potatoes
explode in the microwave
we order pepperoni pizza
and share with Madison.

Other nights
burned eggs
(heat too high)
pasta stuck to the pan
(cooked too long)
even Madison turns up her nose.

Tonight
we try fried chicken.
Dad puts flour and salt and pepper
in a plastic bag

and I shake the bag
until flour covers all the pieces.

I like the sound the chicken makes
when it hits the hot oil
popping and spitting like an angry dragon.

Crunch.
The fried chicken is a success!

Two Months
Minus Mom

Sara Says

Sara wants to be a shrink
so we hang out in her room
listening to CDs
while she tries to figure out
how I should live my life
without my mom.

Sara says,
The first year is the hardest.

"What do you mean?"

Sara says,
*The first time
you go clothes shopping without your mom.
The first time
you get your period without your mom.
The first birthday
you have without your mom.*

I thought I was doing okay
but now I know better

because my stomach jerks
and I run to the bathroom
hold on to the toilet
and try not to think about what Sara said.

Sara says,
It's probably your dad's fault.
He probably made her leave.
She probably wanted to take you
but he wouldn't let her.

Sometimes
Sara says
too much.

I Never Told My Dad

My mom liked to drive fast
especially around corners
where she could jerk the steering wheel
so hard
that even with the seat belt on
my body tipped in her direction.

She called it a C.O.D. curve.
Come over dear
and she'd take one hand off the steering wheel
pull me closer
and kiss the top of my head
laughing so loud that I had to laugh too.

Then she'd ask,
You're weren't scared, were you?

I always said no
but maybe I should have said
yes.

The Note

My teacher sends home a note
about all the homework
I don't do anymore
and all the tests
I don't finish anymore
and how I seem to have
a lot of trouble with my ankle
since I keep missing so much P.E.

I think about leaving it by the coffee pot
so Dad can find it when I'm at Sara's
but instead
I tear it into little pieces
and flush it down the toilet.

Lost

I get a card
with a picture of a white kitten on the front.
Inside it says,
I'm sorry.

No return address.

A stack of mail
with her name on it
waits in a basket on the kitchen counter.

We don't know where to send it.

Every time she calls
she's someplace new
and she hangs up before we can get an address.

I realize Mom is more than gone.
She's lost
and doesn't want to be found.

Sara's House

Sara likes to come over
and help me with my chores
then we watch TV
and talk
about how different my life is from hers.
She likes my house
because it's quiet.

I like it best
when we go to Sara's house
instead of mine
and her mom
wants to hear all about our day
and her big brother teases me
about my long hair and the boyfriends I don't have
and her baby brother sits on my lap
and drools and makes funny faces
and there's so much love in the house
that I think Sara
is the luckiest person in the world.

Not My Mom

Sara's mom
gives big birthday parties
invites all of Sara's friends
orders a huge cake with Sara's favorite frosting
and doesn't care how much noise we make
when Sara opens her presents.

Not my mom.

When I asked for a party
she said no
and that having so many kids in the house
was hard on her.

Sara's mom
likes to play games with us
take us to the movies
and watch us put on skits in the backyard.

Not my mom.

I wanted her to be with me
and she usually wanted to be someplace else.

Sara's mom
lets Sara watch her when she paints
and takes breaks to show Sara how to paint too.

Not my mom.

I wanted to sit with her
when she sat outside with her guitar
but she said the stars
were the only audience she needed.
I would go back to my room and
open the window so I could still hear her sing.

Once I followed her out anyway
(one of her good days)
and she let me stay
and made up a song about a girl named Rachel
who could fly to the moon.

She built a fence around herself
that only let me close enough
to see what I couldn't have.

I wonder if she's happy
now that she's really all alone
all the time.
I wonder if she sits outside somewhere
in her new backyard
strumming her guitar
singing to the only audience she has.

I miss her singing
but not as much
as I thought I would.

Three Months
Minus Mom

Doctor Dan

Every week
we go talk to someone called Doctor Dan.
He's supposed to help us
learn to deal
with Mom leaving us.

I can't make up my mind if I like him or not
but Dad talks more here than at home
and that's good.
I make myself small
in the corner of the big green couch.

Today when he gets to the part
about how he knew Mom didn't want to get married
and how he made her do it anyway
I'm so surprised
I knock a box of tissues off the table
but Dad just keeps talking.

Tell me about that, says Doctor Dan.

I'm glad he asked
what I wanted to know.

I thought she'd grow up and settle down.

Dad looks at me
so I know he knows I'm here.
*She was broken
and I thought I could fix her.*

He talks
and I store up his words
to save for later
when I'm alone in my room.

How Mom got pregnant
and didn't want to keep the baby.
How they fought
and he convinced her to not get rid of it.
How he promised her
everything would be all right
as long as they were together.

Somehow my mind separates
into two places at once
and I don't connect the baby he's talking about
with me.

I think we're done
until Doctor Dan asks him
why it was so important to get married.

I wanted to do the right thing.

He leans forward,
closer to Doctor Dan,
and says,
I loved her.
And as soon as I knew there was a baby,
I loved that baby too.

And suddenly the baby he loved
was me
and the baby that needed two parents
was me
and the baby Mom wanted to get rid of
was me

and I feel like I just jumped off the high dive
and I'm falling
way too fast.

How do you feel about that?
How do you feel about that?
How do you feel about that?

Doctor Dan keeps asking
how do you feel about that?
I keep whispering not so good
then I realize
he's not talking to me.

I look at Dad and think
Doctor Dan is the stupidest man in the world
to keep asking the question
when Dad is breaking in two
right there in front of him.

How do you feel about that?
How do you feel about that?
How do you feel about that?

At first I don't believe it.
He's a rock.
Mom said so.
But Doctor Dan keeps asking him
until I want to jump up and scream for him to
stop
but I don't
and he doesn't stop
until Dad starts to cry.

The Worst Thing

On the way home from Doctor Dan
Dad asks if I'm okay.

I shrug.

Sorry, he says
about what you heard.

I almost convince myself
he made it all up
to keep from telling the real story
then I remember how the rock cracked
right before my eyes
and I know in my gut it's true.

Rachel? We need to talk about this.

I shrug louder.

There's more to the story.
You need to know what it was like,

what your mother was like.
Whenever you're ready, we can talk.

I think I heard enough already.
I think I understand more than I want to.

When Mom left
I didn't think it was possible to feel any worse.
Wrong.
This feels worse.
Much worse.

I shouldn't even be here.
She didn't want me.

She never wanted me.

The Next Worst Thing

This morning
Sara drew a picture on the blackboard
of our teacher Mrs. Duffy
or what Mrs. Duffy would look like
if she weighed 300 pounds and
had an extra eye in the middle of her forehead.

So when the counselor walks into our room
I'm pretty sure I know who she wants.

I feel bad for Sara
because her mom told her
if she got in any more trouble
she'd be grounded for a long time.

Sara slumps in her chair across the room
poking holes in her paper with her pencil.

I'm so busy watching Sara
that I don't hear Mrs. Duffy
the first time she speaks.

Rachel.
The principal wants to see you.
Now.

The Principal's Office

I'm so surprised
I almost shout out a big NO
in the middle of the class.
Then I think about
the note I flushed down the toilet
and the phone messages I never gave to Dad
and I know it's my turn now.

Sara looks like a fish caught on a hook
and everyone stares at me
trying to figure out what I did.
I try to be invisible
but it doesn't work.

I think up excuses as I walk to the office.

It was a dare.
I was possessed by aliens.
I have a rare disease and only six months to live.

I put my hand on the doorknob.
I don't want to go in.

I don't want to have to explain about Mom
and have the principal get that
"I'm so sorry for you" look on her face.
I don't want anyone else to know.

Go on, says the secretary. *She's expecting you.*

I step inside
and come face to face
with the rock.

A Situation

He has on his work clothes
and I wonder what he told his boss
about why he had to leave.
I'm afraid to look at him
so I focus on the colored paper clips
in a glass bowl on the principal's desk.

This can't go on, Rachel, says the principal.
Your father has explained your situation . . .

I don't want to be a situation.
I want to be normal.

You have to participate in class
and do your homework
or you might have to repeat the year.

Dad just sits there and listens
to the principal explain about
the tutoring I have to go to
and the homework notes Dad will have to sign
every night.

When she's through
he stands up
shakes her hand
and thanks her.

Go get your things, Rachel.
You're done for the day.

The Road to Halfway

We drive
past the grocery store
past Sara's house
past the street that takes us home
without talking.

I want to ask where we're going
but I don't want to be the first one to talk.

I hold my backpack on my lap
and slide the zipper
open
and
closed.

He drives through town
almost to the freeway
then home
and doesn't speak
until we're in the house
sitting on opposite ends of the couch.

I don't know what to do, Rachel.

I don't expect this.
Parents are always supposed to know what to do.

Punish you?
More sessions with Doctor Dan?
Maybe Grandma was right.
Maybe she should move in with us for a while.

He waits.
I know he wants me to say something but
I don't know what to do either
so I shrug
and he sighs
and runs his hand over his eyes.

Halfway, Rachel.
You have to meet me halfway on this.
Can you do that?

"Okay," I say.
"I'll try."

Six Months
Minus Mom

Buried Treasure

I have to build a diorama for school
so I ask Dad for a box.
I want to build a big one,
the biggest in the class.

In the garage
the box I want
is home to some of Mom's old books.

I look through the books
about sewing and making candles
and at the bottom I uncover
a photo album and a notebook
held together with a red rubber band.
We both see them at the same time
but he scoops them up first.

I don't recognize the look on his face at first
then I know
it's the same look he had
the day Doctor Dan made him cry.

She told me she threw them away, he says.
She told me she burned them
and threw them away.

Walking back inside
he hugs them to his chest.
I follow right behind.

The Album

Dad sits down at the kitchen table
pulls out a chair for me
and puts the books on the table
between us.

I wait
until he's ready to tell me about them
and the waiting makes my heart beat faster.
Part of me wants to run
but the part of me that wants to know
makes me stay.

He opens the photo album first.
Page one
me
brand newly born
still at the hospital
with my little pink hat
and my arms and legs
all wrapped up tight in a pink blanket.

Page two
me
still at the hospital
where Dad holds me in his arms
smiling down
looking more like a big teddy bear
than any kind of rock.

I've never seen
these pictures
of me and Dad.
Most times
Mom's pictures have red eyes
and the tops of people's heads cut off.
Not these.

Page three and four and more
still me
and Dad.

In the kitchen
where he gives me a bath in the sink.
On the couch
when he feeds me a bottle.

In the yard
where he holds my hand
as I learn how to walk.

Something must be wrong.
I'm pretty sure I've seen pictures
of me with my mom before.
I must have.
But I page through the album three times
and all I see
are pictures of me with Dad.

I look closer now
at one of the pictures inside the house.
It's not our house
it's Grandma's house
Grandma's yard
and even Grandma's kitchen sink
where he gave me my first bath.

The Notebook

I open my mouth to ask
why there are no pictures of me
in *this* house
my house
the only house
I ever remember living in
then he slides the notebook over to me.

Read, he says.

I forget he's there
as I read how Dad and I lived with Grandma
while my mom stayed in a residential hospital
because she had too many problems
to take care of herself
or a newborn baby.
He talks a lot about mental illness
and the psychiatrists Mom talked to
and how they finally figured out
what was wrong with her.

Bipolar disorder.

Suddenly Mom's sickness has a name.
A reason for her mood swings.
A reason for her to fall apart.
A reason for the pills.

I wanted your mom to know
what she was missing, he says,
so I wrote it all down
to share with her later.
Your first steps.
Your first words.
Everything she missed
is in this book.

"In the garage
you were surprised to see it."

We had a fight.
She wanted to hurt me.
She told me she burned it.

He's quiet so long
I don't think he'll say anything else
but he does.

And that's when I told her
to just go ahead
and leave.

Welcome Home

I should be angry
really furious
now that I know he was the one
who told her to go away
but I'm not.

I feel like I've been lost
all my life
and never even knew it
until someone gave me a map
so I could find my way home.

Grandma

Grandma wants to come back
and help
but he tells her no.

You need me, she says.
I can cook and clean and take care of Rachel.

He tells her no
again
in the big voice he uses
to make me clean my room.

Rachel and I need each other.
We can do this, he says.

The Coffee Pot

In the morning
there's a note by the coffee pot.

Have a great day, it says.

And then there's a happy face
where his name should be.

And even though it's raining outside
I dance all the way to school
dodging raindrops
and barely even get wet.

Girl Talk

He wants to talk
about the kinds of things
that I can't talk about
with him.

I tell him
we had a class at school
and he asks,
Is that enough?

I tell him
Sara's mom said
I could talk to her
if I needed to
and he seems happy
to not have to try
to explain
what's hard for a dad to explain.

But the next day
there's a book
about me and my body

on my bed
when I come home from school
and I read it
and I learn some things
I didn't know
and I leave a smiley-face note
for him to find
by the coffee pot.

Conversations

She starts to call every week
and I start to hate
the ringing of the phone.

She never asks how I'm doing
but I tell her anyway
and she talks right over me.

Doing just fine now. No problems at all.
Wrote some new songs,
my best ones yet.
Singing in this lounge on Friday nights.
Could be my big break.

I pretend she listens to me
even though she doesn't wait for me to finish
and each time she ignores me
my heart closes a little bit more.

When she talks to Dad
he doesn't say much either.
Every conversation

ends the same way
with him saying the same thing.

Yes I will. Same as before.

She calls around dinner time.
Always.
Afterward Dad and I push our food around our plates
and end up feeding it to Madison instead.

Tonight when she calls
he's not home.
I hear the panic fill her voice.

Where is he?
The money. What about the money?
I have to talk to him.
Will he send the money?

"What money?" I ask

He promised.
If I called every week he promised to send me money.

Her words cut me
sharper than any knife,
severing another cord
that ties her to me.

I can't swallow.
I can't breathe.

My legs start to shake.
I slide down to the floor
lean back against the wall
and close my eyes.

I want to pretend I didn't hear it.
I want to pretend that she really calls
because she loves me
and she wants to make sure I'm okay
without her.

Now I know better.

I know she just calls
because of some deal she made with Dad

to earn some money for doing her job
of pretending to be my mother.

I want to slam the phone down
but I don't.
I repeat my father's words.

"Nothing has changed."
(I'm glad you're gone.)
"Same as before."
(I don't need you anymore.)

I don't cry
and I'm proud of myself
for learning how to be a rock.

Waiting

This is what I do
after I hang up the phone
while I wait for him to come home:

I wash my face three times
until it looks like I've been running.

I take the picture of Mom and me
out of the frame on my desk
and put in a picture of Madison instead.

I brush Madison's fur
until it shines
and she squirms to get away.

I tug the sock from under my mattress
hold the ring in my hand
and squeeze it tight until it almost hurts.

I shove the sock in the dirty clothes
slam the ring back under the stove
and feel like a rock
when I hear it smack against the back wall.

The Story of Us

Dad finds me
on the couch
my knees pulled up to my chest.
He knows I know.

"Everything," I say.
"Tell me everything.
Don't leave anything out."

He sits close,
but not touching,
and tells me lots of things
I never knew.

About how Mom ran away from home
back in high school
and never saw her parents again.

About the coffeehouse where they met
and where he would listen to her sing.

About her mood swings
that happened
even back then.

She was beautiful
talented
and all mixed up inside.

She needed me
and I needed to be needed.

He reaches out to hold my hand
and I let him.

But when she got pregnant, she didn't tell me.
I tracked her down when she stopped coming to work.
I was afraid she'd run away again.

"She's good at that," I say.

And he doesn't argue with me.

The Rest of the Story

He tells me
how Mom said she wasn't cut out to be a mother
and how he said she could learn
and how they fought about it until Mom gave in.

He tells me
how he promised her
that she could leave whenever she wanted
and how for a long time
she didn't want to.

I figured she'd stayed so long
she'd forgotten about the promise.
I guess I was wrong.
I'm sorry.

And when I look in his eyes
I can see the sorry there
but just because I see it
doesn't mean
I can make all the hurt I'm feeling
go away.

"Why do you send her money?"

I knew how much you'd miss her.
A phone call every week
seemed better than nothing at all.
I guess I was wrong about that too.

"You said she kept you
from getting close to me."

He sighs
and I don't think he wants to answer me
but he does.

It wasn't her, it was me.
I wanted to fix her,
I kept trying to fix her,
but nothing I did ever helped.

I felt like a failure.

And when I couldn't give you the mom you deserved
I just stopped trying.

I chew on my bottom lip
before I ask
the hardest question.

"She never really wanted me, did she?"

He squeezes my hand.
Truth is,
no,
I don't think she ever wanted
to be a wife or a mother.

The hurt
settles in my heart
like one of those giant rocks you tie to something
when you want it to sink
and I feel like I am drowning
in the truth
of his words.

But I wanted you then
and I want you now.

His fingers rub in a circle
on the back of my hand
almost as if he's trying to rub wanting me
into my skin
and make everything all right again.

"She's not coming back is she?"

He reaches for my other hand
and holds them both close in his
as if he's afraid I'm going to disappear.

No, I don't think she is.

Alone in my room
I turn the words over
and over again.

She didn't want to be a mother.
He wanted to be a father.
She didn't want a baby.
He did.
She wanted to leave.
He stayed.

If it weren't for him
I wouldn't be here
or anywhere
at all.

Thank You

I tell him thank you.

For what?

For pretty much everything.

Messages

The next time the phone rings
neither of us rushes to answer it.
She tries seven times
before she finally gives up.

He lets me record a new message
on the answering machine.

"I'm sorry . . ."
(We don't want to talk to you.)

"We aren't able to take your call . . ."
(Because it hurts too much
to think about what you did.)

"If you leave a message . . ."
(Tell us you're sorry
then go away.)

"We'll get back to you as soon as we can."
(Don't hold your breath

because we're building
a new life without you.)

I think about adding thank you for calling
for all the people who aren't her
but I don't.

When I'm done
he puts his hand on my shoulder
and I lean on him
and he leans on me.

It's a good message, he says.
Just perfect.

Cleaning House

She sends a letter asking for
some of the things she left behind.
For once she gives us a return address.

After the boxes are on their way
we clean the house of anything
we don't want to see anymore.

It hurts
but it hurts different.

I guess you're pretty mad at her.

I nod.

*She did the best she could
with what she had in her at the time.*

He says he'll save some things for me
for later
when I'm older
and might want them.

I take Madison for a walk
and when I get back
all traces of Mom are gone
except for the ones you can't see.

Mother's Day

Grandma, Again

Grandma says,
You must need me by now.

Maybe, he says.

Then he adds,
But right now
Rachel and I
we need to be alone together
more.

Father's Day

I'm not sure what the perfect gift is
for a father you've always had
but are just getting to know.

He doesn't hunt
or fish
or bowl
or play golf.

He says he has more ties
than he can wear in this lifetime.

He already has my school picture
on his desk at work.
He showed me once.

I find a peanut butter jar
wash it out
then cover it with blue denim
from an old pair of jeans.
I dig through the photo albums
for a picture of us

and can't find any recent ones
of just me and him.
I finally pick one of the three of us
and use very sharp scissors
to cut Mom out
before I glue the picture
to the jar.

Next I get a piece of paper
so I can write down all the things he does
that make me feel good.
Like the way he lets me make
grilled cheese sandwiches
with burnt cheese around the edges
just the way I like them
even though he can't stand the smell.
And the way he never
says anything rotten about Mom
no matter how many chances I give him.

I tell him it makes me happy
when he tries to tell jokes
and then can't remember the ending

and that it helps a lot when he explains math
with pieces of pizza or chocolate chips.

I tell him not many dads would try to learn Pig Latin
and I like it that he did.

When I'm all done
I cut them into strips,
like the kind inside a fortune cookie,
and stuff them in the jar.

I don't write down
how much I love him
but maybe he can tell
because after he opens it
he puts his hand on my shoulder
and gives it a little squeeze
before he turns away
and rubs his eyes.

Summer Vacation

Dad takes a week off work
and we spend every day
on a new adventure.

We ride the bumper cars
at the amusement park
and spin the Tilt-a-Whirl
until we're both too dizzy to walk.

At the water park
we cover ourselves in suntan lotion
race down the slides
over and over
then end the day on inner tubes
floating in lazy circles.

We go horseback riding
ride our bikes around the reservoir
and eat buttered popcorn
while we watch old movies
late into the night.

The week ends
before I want it to
then he goes back to work
and I go back to hanging out with Sara.

Sara says I look different
but when I check the mirror
I look just the same
to me.

Back to School

Mom always took me shopping
for back-to-school clothes.

We raced from store to store
and she pulled things off the rack
faster than I could try them on.

This year
Dad makes a list
of what I need.

1 new jacket
2 pairs of shoes
sweats for gym
3 shirts
2 pairs of jeans
1 dress (Grandma insists)

I outgrew
almost
all my old clothes.

Do you need a . . . ? he asks.

"A what?"

He mumbles at the floor.

A bra.

I feel my face turn red
hug my arms across my flat chest
and shake my head
no.

Some parts of me
haven't grown
at all.

The Mall

When Dad goes out of town
on a business trip
I spend the night at Sara's house.
He gives me some fun money,
and then some more,
just in case.

Sara and I beg her big brother Sammy
for a trip to the mall
so we can try on clothes
and pretend we're rich
and can buy anything we want.

Sammy wants to get his hair cut
so we wait
sitting in the empty chairs
taking turns spinning each other around.

When it's my turn
I watch in the mirror
as my hair flies out around me

like a cape in the wind
and I get an idea.

I have just enough money.

I sit in the chair
with a real cape around my shoulders
and tell the lady to cut it all off
before I change my mind.

Good-bye Princess

Sara's mom
actually yells at me
about my hair
but I don't care.
I like it short
above my shoulders
with just enough curl
to make it not straight.
I feel different.

Sara says it makes me look older.
Her big brother makes kissing noises
on the back of his hand.
Even Sara's mom says it's pretty
when she finally gets over the shock.

It's easy to comb
and I don't need to braid it
before I go to bed
and I can shake it
real fast
and not make any knots.

But I'm worried about what my dad will say
when he sees it.
Suddenly I want to race back to the hair place
pick up my hair
and glue it all back on.
When he comes to pick me up
I take a long time packing my bag
before I walk out to the living room.

At first
his eyes go real big
and my stomach flips
then he whistles
just like Sara's brother does at his girlfriend
and he tells me I look just like
a movie star.

Me and Doctor Dan

I go see Doctor Dan now
on my own
every Wednesday afternoon.

At first we don't talk about Mom
even though we both know that's why I'm there.
We talk about TV shows
and books
and I tell him I taught Madison
how to play hide-and-go-seek.

I gaze at the colored fish in the tank in the corner.

I think about asking Dad if we can get some fish
even though what I really want is a cat.

Whenever Doctor Dan asks me how I feel
I tell him I don't know
and he says that's okay.

One day I get brave and tell him
I want to hate her

but I can't
and when he says he understands
I feel a little better.

Important Stuff

Dad says I should call him at work
any time it's important
and so I wait for something important to happen
so I can call.

When I get a perfect score on the math test
I think
today's the day.

I'm nervous about calling
and change my mind a bunch of times
before I push the buttons on the phone.

Rachel, what's wrong?

I think maybe this is a stupid idea
and almost hang up.

Rachel? Are you okay? Answer me.

"I'm here. I just called because,
maybe it's dumb,

only we had a math test
and I was the only one
to get all the answers right."

He cheers so loud
it hurts my ears.
I feel all the holes
that Mom's leaving left inside of me
start to fill up with good feelings
and I don't want it to stop.

When he comes home from work
he has all the fixings
for hot fudge sundaes
so we can celebrate
and he doesn't even argue
when I tell him
Madison needs some ice cream too.

Two Weeks Before My Birthday

I wonder if he knows it's coming?
I want to remind him
but I want him to remember on his own.

One Week Before My Birthday

My birthday falls on a Saturday
and I can't decide if that's good or bad.

It's good if he remembers
and we have the whole day to celebrate.
It's bad if he forgets
and I have the whole day to feel miserable.

I look at the calendar
he keeps on his desk
to see if he has anything written
next to my special day.

It's blank.

I think about checking his closet
to see if he has my present hidden there.
What if I find it?

What if I don't?

Happy Birthday to Me

He wakes me
with a knock on my door
and breakfast in bed
just like in the movies.

Madison has on a party hat
there's a candle in my French toast
and I laugh
when he sings Happy Birthday to me
in Pig Latin.

Later he tells me to hurry and get dressed
because we have someplace important to go.

We drive to a part of town
I've never seen
stopping outside a building
where even in the car
I can hear the sound of barking dogs.

Inside
he leads the way to the cat room

and waits patiently while I go from
cage to cage
to pick out just the right one.

There are so many.
I want to take them all home with us
and he reads my mind.

Just one, Rachel, he says.
More than that isn't fair to Madison.

In the very last cage
waits a big orange mama cat and her tiny kitten.
Mama uses her pink tongue
to give her baby a bath.
I stick my fingers through the wire cage.
Mama cat rubs against my finger
purring
while the kitten rubs against the mom
where it's safe.

They belong together
and I want them both.

Seems to me, he says, *that kitten still needs its mom*
and if you want one,
you have to take the other.
Looks like a package deal to me.

"What about Madison?" I ask.

Life's not always fair.
Not for dogs
or cats
or people.

The Truth About Fathers

At school we study all about animal families
how nature adapts
and the animals that survive
are strong in ways the other animals are not.

We read about sharks
and lizards
and how they don't take care of their babies
after they're born.
The babies come out
and have to take care of themselves
or they die.

We watch a film about sea turtles
how they return to the same beach
to lay their eggs and
how the mother turtle returns to the water
before they're even born.

I keep going back
to the stories about animal dads
like the catfish dad

who carries the eggs in his mouth
until they're ready to hatch
going for weeks without food
so he won't accidentally eat any of the eggs.

And the sea horse dad
who keeps the eggs in a special pouch
before he gives birth
to his own babies.

In South America
there's a little monkey called a marmoset.
After the mother gives birth
the father takes care of the baby.
He carries it everywhere
grooms it
brings it to the mother
only at feeding time.
When the baby is ready for solid food
it's the father that feeds it
and makes sure it doesn't starve.

My teacher says it just goes to show
that sometimes
dads are better moms than moms are.

I know she means animals
but I think sometimes
it's true
for people dads too.

Hugging the Rock

We sit on the back porch
and watch the kitten
chase Madison around the yard
while mama cat
suns herself in the middle of the lawn.

Madison stops
barks
and Dad grins when the kitten
scrambles up a tree
leaving Madison behind.

"Are you still mad at Mom for leaving us?" I ask.

I guess some days
I feel worse than others, he says.
How about you?

The kitten climbs down from the tree
and curls up next to mama cat in the sun.
Madison flops on the porch beside me,
and I scratch her ear.

"Some days yes," I tell him,
"but not as much as before."

I feel his arms wrap around me
like this is something we do all the time
and I lean into him.
He hugs me tight
and I realize that some rocks have soft spots
and that I am melting into him
and he holds me
for a very long time.

Year One
Minus Mom

I'm Awake

Rachel, wake up.

I hear his voice in my dreams
but I'm not dreaming.

I'm awake.

He wraps a quilt around my shoulders
and leads me outside.
Madison bounces beside us.

"What's wrong? Is the house on fire?"

No, he says, *it's the sky.*
The sky is on fire.

He keeps his arm around me and points up.

A meteor shower. I didn't want you to miss it.
Watch, he whispers.

We sit
snuggled close beneath the quilt.
It's very dark
the sky is crystal clear
and suddenly it's like the Fourth of July
with a sky full of sparklers.
It's beautiful.

I expect to hear a pop and sizzle
as they explode above us
but it's quiet,
a good time for thinking.

And I think of how far we've come
since Mom ran away
and how Mom was right.
He is a rock,
the kind you can count on
to do all the right things
like staying
when other people want to run
and like waking me up
so I don't miss the shower of stars
in the middle of the night.

Acknowledgments

Thank you to my wonderful critique group: Bonny Becker, Susan Heyboer O'Keefe, and Laura Purdie Salas. Whenever I was afraid to step outside my comfort zone, you held my hand and told me I could do it.

I appreciate the many readers of this story along the way: Janie Bynum and Jane Buchanan, who read the first poems and told me to keep going; Patricia Thomas, Lissa Halls Johnson, and Dandi Daley Mackall, who pushed me to continue to tell the truth; Toni Buzzeo, the sister of my heart; and a special thank you to Janet Wong, who first suggested I play with poems and see where they took me and my characters. You helped me find my voice. Karen Grencik was steadfast in her support for this story, and my agent, Jodi Reamer, was a true champion. Thank you.

A big group hug to everyone on the Pod who has kept me afloat emotionally for many years. Thanks for always listening and loving me through it all.

A very special thanks to my fabulous editor, Nicole Geiger, who kept asking tough questions until I dug deep enough to reach the heart of the characters. With a gentle hand you pulled out individual story threads and asked me to rethink, revise, and sometimes even (gasp) throw things away, making a book that is not only stronger and more authentic, but one that brings to life the story I wanted to tell.